Life Before

Also by Stephen Outram

Books:
The First Five Years: Port Hedland 1965-1970
Wedding Speeches
Dealers: Buying, Selling & Making Money
Public Speaking: Beyond Fear
Advanced Speaking Concepts
There's No Sex in Golf
Life After

Will Public Speaking Be The Death of You? (OOP)

Blog & Articles:
stephenoutram.com

Life Before

By Stephen Outram

Author: Stephen Outram

Date Published: August 2008

ISBN: 978-0-9943327-0-7

Publisher: What Else is Possible?
PO Box 1770, Broadbeach, QLD. 4218. Australia

Contents

Introduction

I hope you enjoy this collection of writings that have emerged over the years.

Many lived in dark cupboards on scraps of paper until I became aware that they would actually like to be read. Words, it seems, have a life and desires of their own; and who am I to deny them and you the possibility of enjoying each other.

How many poems and writings are there, living in draws and cupboards all over the world that would like to be set free? Perhaps you might find some of your own and dust them off. What would that be like and what else can you create?

Of Poetry

Be still.

Experience poetry without hurry and in comfort lest you miss the beating of your heart or the stirring of your soul.

Read out loud and gift space the beauty of your voice and the sweet warmth of your breath.

Speak from being, that you may discover more of you than you could ever imagine. Be you and color what you say with everything you are.

Know the power of words, perceive their energy, receive their vibration with ease and be aware of where they touch you.

Listen closely and be present, for someone truly extraordinary is speaking.

White They Crack

Sharp they tack, sails on fire,
Bursting with light and air; humming wire.
White they crack and beat the sky,
The rudder bites; they fill and sigh.

Stretched taunt, full and rich,
Pulling hard, she leans, they twitch.
Over to port, the sheets white with strain,
Stays strung tight; wind's abeam.

Around she goes, gasp for air,
Out tumbles the wind; captain's despair.
Around she comes, the turn is true
And white they crack; tails askew.

To fill once more and test the mast,
Taking the strain,it holds them fast.
Cup the wind, they puff and fill,
Driving her through the westerly swell.

Forward they press, the bow's a knife;
A rainbow's spray, 'tis a sailor's life.

Ah, The Wind

Ah, the wind
That fills lungs then snatches warm breath away;
Teasing ears with words unknown,
Speaking the language of Earth
And singing to hearts.

The wind at play, the wind on high,
The wind a howl or gentle sigh.
The wind in flight, a seamless bound;
The wind it shrieks, a soundless sound;
The wind that carves, reshapes and builds.
The wind that dies and is reborn;
Lost to eyes though the skin knows its form.

The breathless wind, the wind at play;
Waving flags and sailing clouds;
Speaking softly then crying out loud.
Flickering flames, ember's tease;
A sailor's friend, the wind a breeze.

The soundless wind, can be heard still;
The laughing wind it teases.
The constant wind, known so well;
That ever-changing wind yet somehow, the wind still.

Fisher Folk

The fisher folk came by this morn,
Wearing white and cloaked in dawn.
Accent the grey, dark the brown;
Closely fitted, a feathered gown.

The early light had barely caressed the sky,
As fisher folk came on by.
Stealthy on the morning tide,
Across still water silhouettes glide,
Along the shore where the weed did lie,
Fisher folk sailed on by.

A bright eye glanced me where I sat
And passed me over.
"Good morning Sir," my mind offered;
Though no reply could I gather.
Subtle ripples trailed the craft,
As the hunter turned and motored past;
Noiseless, sleek rod held high,
The fisher folk glided by.

A silver flash beneath the glass;
Rod cocked ready for the cast.
Muscles coiled, building the strike;
Again, tantalizing, a flash of light.
Time suspended, focus, adjust the throw;
Then shattering the mirror, pink spear is thrust below.

Bubbles rise and forge escape;
Though not the catch, patiently we wait.
The pregnant trap is slowly withdrawn,
As the mirror heals; still we wait.
Finally then, filter the prize, retain the prey;
The fisher folk eat well today.

Stillness returns, a moment has passed;
The distorted reflection wobbles then gathers itself.
Revealing a long sharp spear of a beak,
Where pink fleshy jowls hang lose in repose;
An elegant tapered neck carries small head.
A bright eye glances me again;
I nod as the fisher folk paddle by,
Another place their luck to try.

Birthdays

Birthdays can be special events; celebrations of the day you were born. And what a wonderful day it was when you chose to join the rabble of humankind on Earth.

What blessing did you share with the world when you took your very first breath and sweetened the air with the unique sound of your voice?

What joy did you bring to those waiting? Given freely with no thought of return; a gift of the heart.

And the light, that brilliant light that blazed into the world when you first opened your eyes. Light that has blazed ever since; washing over all who stand before you drawn like moths, dazzled by the possibility that you are.

Birthdays can special events, celebrations of the day you were born; the day the world changed and was never the same again. That day the world was a different space; that special and wonderful day when you were born and a new possibility came into being.

Mrs. Whittey

I'm not sure why she died,
Mrs. Whittey;
Maybe she just got old.

I only saw the people gathered at her grave.
Through the window I saw them;
My mother said, "Don't look son"
And pulled the curtain closed.

I thought about the friend I'd lost;
I should have been there as they lowered her body into
the ground,
To say my good-byes, as the others did.

I had a right to say goodbye;
For she had been kind to an eight year old,
Mrs. Whittey.

I loved her in my youthful way
And now, at forty years I still remember her kindness,
To a young migrant boy short of grandmothers.

So, for what I didn't say then I say it now,
Goodbye Mrs. Whittey.
God bless Mrs. Whittey.
Thank you for being my friend.

Stephen Outram

The Life of Candles

Candles flicker,
Their halos glow softly,
The waxen markers of time do they bare.

The light of their giving,
Mirrors their essence,
A soft gentle stillness, auras golden, beauty rare.

Slowly transforming,
They change their expression,
Shedding the rigid bodies they show.

In exchange,
For the flame of their knowing,
The glory and grandeur of the light that they throw.

Until molten and liquid,
The last of the body,
Gives fuel to the light and warmth to the air.

Feeble and dying,
Now but a teardrop,
Exchanged for the ether; transformed in the flare.

The light all but gone now,
The warmth barely a whisper,
Given in glory; a final glimpse of gold.

Until at last extinguished,
A wisp of smoke slowly rising,
Returns to the universe; becomes one with the all.

As the life of a man or a flower or a bird or an hour,
The life of a candle, a mirror, a reminder of the cycles of
power.
For in all things a pattern is seen;
Creation's hand revealed, in light's naked sheen.

Dog's Smile

Dogs appear to smile when they're happy. It's not a big toothy grin that gives it away; a dog smiles with its whole body. Every part from nose to tail is used to express its joy. A dog doesn't hide or conceal what it's being and why would it want to? For in expressing its joy so fully, the dog gives away and shares that with whoever is willing to receive it.

Who could resist the temptation to smile when watching dogs play in the surf and come away uplifted? Similar, the open inventive games of children; unconcerned with outcomes or expectations, they play without inhibitions, just being children, effortlessly.

How wonderful for we adults, who often need such skilful teachers.

Message To Sheryl

You are beautiful.
And when I merged with you
I was filled your beauty and your peace.

And though I planned to gift,
Upon withdrawing,
It was I who was replete with your sweetness.

Thank you.

Peace

Peace.
And within that peace something else;
A subtle activity,
A barely discernible hum.
Listen, at a new level,
With greater awareness and presence.

Peace.
And within that peace an absence of the greater noise.
Revealing a softer vibration;
Finer and lighter.

Peel-back the layers and discover anew,
Other expressions of lives and living;
Other worlds,
Another universe.

Peel-back your own layers;
You are more than you think,
More than you perceive.

Look deeper to realize; what?
All that you are.
Take your time;
Your whole lifetime.

Peace.
And within peace there is much to hear; much to know;
For those who will listen;
For those who sit,
Silently, in peace.[1]

---

1   In July 2000, I visited Chenrezig Institute,;a Buddhist
centre located near Eudlo in southeast Queensland, Australia. It is
a most beautiful place. While sitting in the sun trying to read I was
distracted; I heard a soft hum and saw a small flying insect hover
in the air above the lawn. Fascinated, I concentrated and became
aware of the subtle sounds of many other tiny creatures. I had never
heard these sounds in this way before and putting down my book,
listened; such is the peace of Chenrezig.

An Essay on Sunlight

"Speak to me of sunlight," I asked, bathing in its dewy goldenness while lazing upon a comfortable rock at the ocean's edge, under the blue canopy of a clear winter sky.

Sunlight is the light of the sun; in relation to your planet's solar system it is the greatest source of light you perceive. The sun, as light's source in your world, symbolizes the source of all light in a total system: light that is infinitely small or large, brilliant or dark; it is thought, simply, to be all that there is.

Everything that is in the *greater* is present in the *lesser*; the reverse is also true. Therefore, everything is everywhere all of the time. In this way, sunlight is all-light and no-light; it is brilliance and darkness, and as the candle's shadow is never apart from the flame, dark is not separate from light. Thus, it follows, that night is never separate from day and you can observe that one follows the other in perpetually and both exist at the same time on Earth.

Your physical location on the planet's surface determines which you perceive. Therefore, your experience of light or dark, day or night, is related to your location. In using the vehicles of time and motion you can remain within the sun's light as long as your motion is sustained. If you used motion—travelling with the rotation of Earth—to remain in light, then your experience of dark would be nil. This activity, however, does not negate the possibility and the reality of dark; it merely speaks of your current, limited experience.

This reasoning suggests there may be other forms of light and dark which humans do not perceive, though may exist, and points clearly to the fact that your experience of sunlight is a result of an ability to perceive its existence on one, more, or many levels within all that there is.

Enjoy sunlight, for it is one of your planet's many wonders. As you sit, basking, receiving its nurturing qualities, become aware that in the extreme it also has the ability to destroy life. Within the range of its existence, life-giving is balanced with life-taking. Further investigation will reveal that all things can contribute to or take away from life. And at the extreme edges of their range, extreme awareness is required.

Stephen Outram

Thus, life, experienced with sunlight is most pleasant
and beneficial when in harmony and balanced with
darkness; and so it is that the only way to know both
light and dark simultaneously is in their extreme range.
For in ultimate dark, light exists and in ultimate light,
dark exists; they are coexistent. Be aware, however, that
both life and death also exist within a similar idea of
polarity as do all things, within all that there is.

And so, for some, the experience of sunlight is simple:
it comes, it goes and is replaced by night. Nothing more
is required to be known. Yet within this discussion,
we have touched upon many things that are available
within all that there is. It would appear that one's
experience of sunlight or anything, is based in choosing
the range of awareness that satisfies the seeker.
Experience itself, then, is provided within a chosen
range even thought the available range may be zero to
infinity, which are extremes and therefore reach out to
one another. This suggests the cyclical nature of things;
each returning to its beginning, or end, in perpetually;
as light-to-dark and dark-to-light.

That which we have been calling a range, may be
described by some as a journey and some might
call it adventure; it's part of your experience of
somewhere between zero and infinity. The adventure
of experiencing sunlight becomes a reality to be found
between the simple and complex, zero and infinity, or
just sitting on a rock in the afternoon's golden light.

Paths

Many are the pathways and roadways of life;
They wind and turn and twist confusingly.
Yet, like a maze, there is but one way
And the journey unfolds to reveal that surely in the
linearity of time.

Travel with ease,
Knowing that the way is always before you;
Awaiting your foot steps and
Rejoicing in your tread.
The path, but a servant,
Shines as gold when its purpose is revealed.

For the journey can be chosen
And choice creates.
Choose and create your journey,
And watch the pathway unfold before you.

September 11

Hard it came and fast,
The news they bore to me.
Comprehending it too thorny a task,
My mind rejecting the improbability.
My heart unable to accept the loss,
Staggered, and for a moment it stilled

Huge; it was immense, so large.
I didn't believe, could not accept;
I cried disbelief and rejected its import.
I cast it aside to look for the sun through the dust,
But nowhere could I find the light;
Only dark.

And still they came and persevered,
To impress upon my mind the facts.
In many forms to my eyes and my ears;
They screamed in my face, until …
I had no choice, but to accept, for it was real.

My shield was shattered as the many lives,
My heart broken as the toppled walls,
My mind scarred as the ruined land,
My soul burnt as the flames claimed it,
My life changed as the landscape;
Now dark with blood and death.

I tower no more, I am reduced in my sadness;
Crumpled and shapeless, a ruin, the dark grave.

And then, a tear, God let me grieve;
But she is silent, waiting, watching.
For only I may allow it, this grief.
And anger, I feel it
Rising, enormous, raging, choking pressure.

Again, a tear, please God help me;
Still he is silent, waiting, watching.
Silently I weep until I find voice and sob,
To grieve at last.

And to grasp cautiously at life once more;
Tiny, shaking steps do I take.
I see you there, silent, waiting, watching;
Wait, I am coming;
Yes, finally, I am here.

Beyond The Veil

Formless, cloudless, a sky of blue seeps into my room transforming the view. Washed in watercolor, a pigment of my imagination brushes the horizon with soft indigo hues.

Gathered there within its tresses, subdued, sublime, a toneless veneer drifts amongst life's soulful caresses. A glamour, a glimmer, a magick, a veil.

Past this containment I seek to travel, through its delightful enticing form; it holds me though with illusional splendor. I fail to see beyond the flimsy that surrounds and stimulates my every perception, creating me an individual, apart from everything there is.

Can I move past sense and reason to be free flying beyond these perceptual prisons, again to be one? For this I yearn at levels deeper than worldly sensation. A knowing tugs, a pain, a spell, something deeply embedded that conveys subtly a promise; the Veil to dispel.

Away from thoughts and feelings of hunger, removed from the dust and the glare and the noise. Revealed in the peace of meditation a oneness that has always been there.

A promise fulfilled, questions now answered and mysteries dissolve with time's fading hold. Oneness, the oneness, the completeness, the wholeness; no longer fragmented, a knowing of all. A joyful reunion; united at last, to realize in that instant I've always been part.

The veil that curtains and cloaks now vanishing, like mist before the morning sun. I see the matrix woven tight, a pattern expanding, an unending vision of radiant light.

And there I am everywhere; there is nowhere I am not; my individual illusion, my separateness revealed false. For hidden within the veil's apparent seclusion, I have found me at last.

Little Birds

Little birds don't take much space,
They require just a little place.
Filled with light and air and seed,
Is all a little bird does need.
And to leap up into the great big sky,
Where little birds love to fly.

Little birds love their mates
And all agree that trees are great.
Little birds sing so sweet
And get around on little feet.
That leap into the great big sky,
Where little birds love to fly.

We are all little birds at heart,
Though sometimes we forget the art;
Of leaping into the great big sky,
Where little birds just love to fly.

Fairy Delight

Creeping, crying, Taliesin rhyming;
Light-lustred horses, bright fairies driving.
Mushrooms and toadstools, their proud voices singing
Chants of the ancients, the spells they be bringing

Castles 'gainst darkness, battlements a glowing;
Pennants and flags, their banners be flowing.
Lighted and flickering the torches they bear
That shine on the darkness and dance in the air.

Merlin and magic, palaces and kings;
Earthly concoctions, enchantment and things.
Magical moments, mysteries unfold;
Movement and gesture, timeless resolve.

Priests in their pulpits, murmurings of heart;
Golden light-forms, expressions of art.
Mystical music, soft weaving flow;
Choirs enrapture, gilded notes grow.

Mid summer night's party, not far from here;
Deep in the garden, lost to our ear.
Delicate and joyful, soft in the night;
Right on our doorstep, lost in our sight.

Stephen Outram

Felt in our hearts though, their laughter; delicate, tiny
and bright.
Found in our hearts, the twinkling of fairy delight.
Right on our doorstep, they reach out to us so;
To find when they touch us, in our hearts, that we know.

Light Always Shines

Three battle-weary soldiers sat around a large refectory table in a room, smoking their cigarettes and softly talking.

The first, who was in a very depressed state, spoke of the battlefield, of blood, death and the grave.

The second soldier; his leg had been amputated. He spoke of loss: the loss of self-esteem, missing comrades and friends, the loss of his leg and with it his confidence.

The third soldier was silent. He sat watching the light that streamed in through an open window; its curtains moving gently in the air. He watched how the light's rays played across the furniture and walls, creating shadow and dimension, influencing everything with color and energy

Gradually, the three men disappeared; each lost in their own thoughts and the room fell silent. The light continued to shine into the room, carrying on with its games.

After a time the sun began to set, deepening the shadows. Out of its last dying flames, however, the moon rose and was reborn into the night sky. Her pristine light crept through the open window and soon the room was awash with silver.

Stephen Outram

As the moon rose higher in the sky the room changed again; becoming brighter as the light played, creating subtle diffuse shadows and a surreal sense of dimension.

Eventually the moon rolled out of view and was unable to deliver its light through the window.

The moon's absence served only to make the glittering stars more apparent and the splendid light that they shone into the room; light so old as to be unmeasurable, that had journeyed from stars so numerous as to be uncountable and it was glorious.

We are reminded that light all ways shines, though in many guises; that light will all ways flow into open hearts as open windows and is there whether we are aware of it or not.

The bounty of life is all around though, often, one must look beyond troubles that seem so solid and real and see them in a different light.

The Joys of Life

Cause yourself to wonder, on the fragrance of a flower;
Allow yourself to feel the breeze that strokes your hair.
Quiver a little, at the awesome power of thunder,
And listen to the ocean in the conch of a shell.

The wind at play in meadows, sunshine through the
trees,
Moonlight on the water rippled by a breeze,
The dancing sparkle of water alight, starlight's journey
through the night;
The silent wonder of knowing eternity in a day.

These are things that make me smile,
These are things that enchant my mind,
These are things that delight my soul,
These are things that make me whole.

So many things that I adore
And still to name, so many more.
The joys of life, I love them all;
It seems from heaven that they fall.

Lanterns

Lanterns unguarded,
Their lights bursting outward,
Guide us in darkness and lighten our footsteps where
willing hearts go.

Their movement and flicker,
Dance soft on our pathways;
The comings and goings of life do they show.

And pathways that lead us,
Should we choose to follow,
That guide us in search of life's gentle flow.

As flickering lanterns,
Cast out the shadows,
And colour our way with their soft gentle glow.

Coloring

Colored blinds and columbines;
Ribbons ragged, twining with elastic paper shapes.
Dabs of paint;
Smears of shapeless hue, lines to nowhere, or
somewhere.
Do you remember you at their age?
Fantasy and delight; dabbling in art.

The colour wheel, paint mixing lessons and other
structures; who needs 'em?
A splash of this and that, whatever is near—the wall, a
door; each a viable canvas.

"I need more space; art on walls has been known to last
hundreds of years!"

"Not in this house." says Mum.

So, what's next?
Crayons, textas, paint—acrylic and water.

"More paper; my fingers are burning. They seem to have
a life of their own."

Where does this stuff come from? From me?

Reds and blues, rainbows and oceans, mountains and
forests. Monkeys:

"Look, there's Dad! He-he. Oops! Sorry, it's an abstract monkey Dad now."

Where will it all end? How did it start? Will it ever end? I hope not.

Walls covered with pieces of paper coloured by children; galleries of wealth.
And happy parents sharing these patches of sunlight; splashes of color and creation.
Remembering the fun and joy of youthful expression.
Color without limits or guidelines. No limits. Limitless.

Color has no limits.
When did the limits start?
Where did the color go?

"I'd forgotten how much I like coloring." says Mum.

Feather Pillows

Soft, softly, softest;
Feathers, down and fluff.
Filling my pillows;
Filling my sleep.

Rest, resting, rested.
Such fine pillows;
Rest on my bed,
Awaiting my weary head.

Sleep, sleeping, slept;
Warm, soft and deep.
Of my slumber,
My mornings
And of my dreams.

Dream, dreaming, dreamt;
Of ducks, swans and geese,
Flying into my pillows,
As I sleep.

Soft, softly, softest;
Feathers, down and fluff.

A Tale of Three Cats

The tale of three cats is sublime.
A pad and the purr,
A hidden rapier;
Furrr.

Stretch and yawn,
A cursory lick;
The softest of coats
And a tail.

A tale of three cats;
Misleading it seems.
A tail of three cats.
Three cat tails;
Three cats.
Such a tale.

Fare Ye Bright

On winded fare, "Knoll fell." said she ...

There came a man that princely day,
Tall and forlorn was his way.
With pride his passion and hope his sword,
Be he stately prince or sovereign lord.

Delivered into this place he went,
Head held high though shoulders bent;
And farther than anyone had gone,
He ventured forth as if a storm.

The torrent winds they tore his cloak
And battered his person till it felt broke;
A twisting turning vex came
And lay heavy on his heart.

Till shining light his eye did catch;
A twinkling point, a burst, a shaft.
This princely light his eyes did seek,
At yon illuminati was his peace.

And so he strode, oh forward go,
Ye sovereign King, ye light aglow;
Strive amongst the tempest storm.
The time of your coming delights and warms all lonely
souls.

Stephen Outram

Behest along your way,
The gift of light drawn from the day.
A cast into the night,
A pearl of glowing light.
Till all aglow delights an aching heart or weary brow.

Such wisdom is for all to sow,
Into the hearts of those and yon.
Speed it to the hearts where just belongs.
For rainy comes and rainy goes from the heart of thee
that knows.

Such simple wisdom err it seems,
Just beyond a glimpse immortal realms
And graceful as a silvered swan,
Will guide the light where just belongs.

Caressing, graceful, such timely light,
A pearl of wisdom, a sacred sight.
Deflowers and defrocks ye, faithful go,
Pathways and byways that ye know.

Take a turn and sight the bend,
In every life behold the end.
Of physical purpose and worldly things.
Then drawn upwards enlightened springs the soul, she
dances on golden wings.

Returns at last this day,
The bosom of that earthly plane releases just,
It is reborn.
Ken tell if yon or here.

The bursting light is all to bear,
The brilliant light is all to bear,
The guiding light is all to bear,
And one with all the brightest prayer.

Time, the Eternal Question

There is time in a life,
Just as time in a day,
The passing of time,
Just passing away.
Where does it go
And why won't it stay?
The illusive mystery
Of time in a day.

The ticking of clocks,
Signal moments of now;
That are here for a moment
And then gone somehow.
As if called then abandoned,
Discarded or lost,
To be replaced with another;
It all happens so fast.

Speed blurs the distinction,
Between this moment and next.
It seems a seamless motion,
Perpetual unrest.
Flowing, rhythmic;
Cycles beyond the range of our grasp;
The life of a moment
Eludes our senses and quickly becomes past.

But in the moment of its creation,
From where did a moment spring?
What energy did conceive it,
Give it birth, make it sing?
And in the moment of it's passing,
Before the next bursts into view;
Is there a moment between the moments,
A place that creates a moment anew?

And if its there,
How do we mark it?
Is it beyond our system of time?
If it's there,
How will we know it,
With no measure we can define?

Perhaps time, in its passing,
Doesn't really pass us by?
Perhaps we move through its stillness,
Unaware it is we who fly.
Thinking that we are bound
By time's symbolic tick-tock;
When in fact, we are timeless
And hold the keys to its crusty lock.

Who knows this mystery,
Who's mind can we ask?
The brows that time furrows,
With this puzzle, this quandary, this task.
It continues unaffected
By anything we say, do or dream;
As we strive to unravel
The measured treads, of time's illusive scheme.

Gardens

The seeds of our dreaming,
The cry's of our longing,
Endeavour to guide us
Thought lonely they grow.

From season to season,
Err ever-splendid,
Fallen petals of flowers
Cast down in the snow.

Yet in the springs of each lifetime,
Seeds that journey through darkness,
Shoot up in our hearts;
Feelings that grow.

To bloom in our summers
And fade in our autumn's,
Then sleep through our winters;
Such gardens we sow.

Autumn's Forest

Have you ever walked through autumn's forest
And kicked the leaves with your feet.
Felt the cold breath of change
Whispering softly against your cheek.
Have you brushed the leaves from your hair
And watched them tumble to the ground.
To settle gently on the patchwork fabric
Of autumn's auburn gown.

Have you sailed through autumn's forest
To chart the rustic leafy sea.
Seen the sparkle of golden rays
Reckless through the torn and fragile canopy.
Have you touched the bared limbs of brothers-in-arms,
Keeping their secrets still;
Who having shared summer's weight,
Now stand-alone and reflect on winter's chill.

You can find peace in a forest
With the leaves now settled and still;
Their frenzied flight now sated
As if by a lover's skill.
And though you feel alone listen,
And hear the muted sounds.
Of slumbering souls awaiting the time when again,
Their profusion of wealth will abound.

Stephen Outram

I found love in autumn's forest
As I wondered aimless through the trees.
She came to me shyly
And gently touched me with autumn's scented breeze.
I felt her kiss my mouth and touch my heart,
Her embrace a playful squeeze.
She held me with her charms and spells,
A love borne of wishing wells,
Now only memory dwells,
Beneath the naked trees.

A lonely crow calls staccato
Through a grey and leadened sky.
A moment's hesitation, then black-feathered wing-tips
Brush chill surprise.
Soft misty rain settles on my skin,
Goose bumps raise the reply.

It is time to leave,
I turn to go.
One last look,
This place I know.
The turning seasons,
Cycles in flow;
Goodbye autumn, goodbye.

About The Author

Biography

Stephen Outram has a background of some eighteen years in architecture, and since 1997 has worked as a graphic artist, website developer and Internet consultant. More recently he is a writer and seminar presenter.

His family emigrated to Australia, from England in 1965, landing in Fremantle and spending five years in the northerly town of Port Hedland. In 1970 the family drove across the country from west to east and settled in Queensland's Gold Coast, where his parents and sister still reside. Educated in Queensland, Australia, Stephen studied at Brisbane's University of Technology in the early 1970s; he returned to study in 1995 at Dundee University, Scotland, achieving a Master of Science degree in Computing.

Stephen enjoys a diverse and wide range of projects including work, writing, music and song writing, boats and some sport. He is active with Surfrider Foundation Australia and is interested in sustainable and flourishing coastlines and waterways, free of plastics and pollution.

Visit the website for more information visit stephenoutram.com

Other Books

By Stephen Outram

The First Five Years: Port Hedland 1965-1970

Imagine leaving everything you know—your job, family, friends; your country—and setting off on a journey that will take you 20,000 km across the planet to a remote, isolated town where you are not known, have no job and must begin creating your life; would you do it?

> "This is brilliant scene setting; what was then, what had been and when you guys arrived, it was just awakening. Awesome story telling! I am still intrigued and want to read more."

> "Every time I read this I am amazed by the 'Yes!' attitude and zest for life."

Stephen Outram's new book, The First Five Years, tells the true story of a small English family that left home to go and forge a new life in Australia. Their first five years in the small, isolated town of Port Hedland, which regularly experienced searing heat, cyclones and offered very basic facilities, required courage, guts and the willingness to do whatever it took and not give up on their dreams.

Wedding Speeches

For many, being asked to give a Wedding Speech is the first time they will speak to a larger group, and these speeches may be done only once in a lifetime. Copying and pasting someone else's lines off the Internet is just not good enough. This book will assist you in creating your speech, with ease!

Professional speaker and coach Stephen Outram connects you with everything you need, to accomplish what may be one of the most important speeches of your life!

- Discover a simple idea with 3 parts and begin organizing and preparing your Wedding Speech.

- How to convert what's in your head, into a vital resource.

- Detail descriptions of the 5 key wedding speeches, including the Bride's Speech—a woman's role in transforming long-standing traditions

- The real job of a wedding speech and your role in accomplishing it

- 9 things that you may have to handle that no one tells you about!

Over 80 pages of information, ideas and techniques, designed to assist anyone who has been asked to give a Wedding Speech.

More information at stephenoutram.com

Dealers: Buying, Selling & Making Money

Dealers are people who can make things move! They are market creators and facilitate the flow of ideas, objects and objectives, connecting sellers and buyers. Dealers make money as a consequence of their ability to move energy and create results.

The ideas, concepts and tools that this book contains will connect you with the dealer that you have always wanted to be, but have not yet been introduced to; until now!

- What deals you will not walk away from that are costing you more than you know?

- The 5 key characters that you need, to be a dealer and make money.

- Are you speculating about making money rather than making money speculating?

- What is BIRGing and are you using it to disadvantage?

- Do your investments resemble losing football clubs that you loyally support with your money?

Treasure Hunter, Collector, Bargainer, Speculator and Investor—which are you using to your disadvantage and how do you turn that around?

More information at stephenoutram.com

Public Speaking: Beyond Fear

Public Speaking: Beyond Fear is designed for people who experience difficulty with public speaking and performance. It will also benefit people who think they have it all handled.

The ideas, concepts and tools contained in this book may catapult you to levels of freedom and ease with public speaking that you've never had before.

- Begin functioning beyond normal

- Discover why anxiety is your best friend

- The weird, hidden issues that you can change

- The Art of Public Speaking explained

- Understanding Fight-Flight and working with your body

- Why amateur speakers never get paid

What if your journey with public speaking was really an adventure, unfolding before you with each new choice you make?

More information at stephenoutram.com

Advanced Speaking Concepts

Advanced Speaking Concepts is written for people who are seeking to create something greater and something different with public speaking. It will also benefit people who are beginning; the new generation of speakers.

This book contains ideas and concepts to assist you going beyond all of the old, worn public speaking techniques that everyone else uses to be competent, average and safe.

- Exposed! The myth that public speaking is the No.1 fear.

- The weird and hidden issues that are holding you back.

- Nerves! Why you need them to perform better.

- Applause. A beginning, not the end.

- Manipulation! Using it to advantage.

What if your journey with public speaking was really an adventure unfolding before you with each new choice you make?

More information at stephenoutram.com

There's No Sex in Golf

This is golf beyond the mental game; looking at all of the hidden places and spaces that players use to limit what's possible with their game, and are totally unaware of it.

Imagine that you have been playing golf with a group of mates for several years; you're one of the gang and a trusted member. You all meet up every Saturday for the club competition, lose, but socialise in the bar afterwards as good mates do. What would happen if you allowed your game to improve dramatically and began winning; not just once but again and again? This is similar to someone who suddenly becomes wealthy and their friends or family become very uncomfortable when confronted with the new diamonds, BMW and beachfront mansion. Back to golf—are you unconsciously using your peer group as a reason to not play your best game and continue improving beyond their wildest imaginings?

There's No Sex in Golf is a book that addresses golf beyond the mental game, and probes into the sometimes sensitive nooks and crannies that golfers may not want to look at. What are the hidden techniques that golfers use so effectively that they can't get past them to play their best golf?

Unlike most other golf books, There's No Sex In Golf has little to say about your swing or what you need to fix or eliminate from your game. It does ask you, however, to look at your game from a different perspective and get clear on what you're really creating with golf and what else you could be choosing.

More information at stephenoutram.com

www.ingramcontent.com/pod-product-compliance
Lightning Source LLC
Chambersburg PA
CBHW050906120626
46554CB00003B/1048